THE EAST PUDDING CHRONICLES
The Christmas Monster

To Billie,
Merry
Christmas!

CR.Berry

X

The East Pudding Chronicles

THE CHRISTMAS MONSTER

WRITTEN BY

CHRISTOPHER BERRY

ILLUSTRATED BY EMILY HARPER

Printed in the UK by Lulu.com

ISBN 978-1-4478-9999-0

For all my Berries

THE EAST PUDDING CHRONICLES
The Christmas Monster

Chapter One
Granny Tells a Story

It was the night before Christmas in a little village called Dandiest Pug. In a cosy house on the corner of Cherry Street, Granny was busy in the kitchen making spicy cookies. The strong, sweet, Christmassy smell of cinnamon wafted out of the kitchen into the rest of the house.

Dipstick the naughty puppy was running around Granny's feet with a squeaky ball in his mouth. All of a sudden, he ran straight into Granny's ankles, jogging her as she poured flour into her mixing bowl. A puff of flour floated to the kitchen floor, tickling Dipstick's nose and making him sneeze.

Dipstick charged into the living room, where George and Georgina were sitting by the window, watching the snow outside.

Their Mum and Dad had gone out for Christmas Eve drinks, and Granny was babysitting and getting everything ready for Christmas Day. Not long now, George and Georgina thought as they watched the snow-filled sky. Not long till Santa Claus gets here.

They spun round when they heard Dipstick smack straight into the Christmas tree behind them, sending a wave of little snowman-shaped chocolates flying across the room. Georgina laughed.

"Granny, he's done it again!" George shouted to Granny, who was still busy in the kitchen. She had cut lots of Christmassy shapes out of her cookie dough and put the cookies in the oven. She washed her flour-dusted hands under the tap and went into the living room.

"Dipstick! Naughty dog!" Granny scolded. Dipstick stood in the centre of the living room with wide, excited eyes, still squeezing the squeaky ball in his grinning mouth. If dogs can grin, that is. His tail was wagging too, so he certainly wasn't feeling bad about having knocked all the chocolates off the Christmas tree, which was still wobbling from side to side. George and Georgina giggled.

"Deary me!" Granny cried, bending down to cuddle the cheeky puppy. "I just can't stay angry at you! Not when you look at me with those eyes!" Granny smiled, sighed and went to sit in her armchair.

"Is everything ready for Santa, children?" she asked George and Georgina.

Georgina looked at the fireplace. The fire had gone out, leaving behind just a few logs half-eaten by the fire and lots of little piles of black ash.

"Well the fire's gone out. So the fireplace is safe for Santa's bottom when he comes down the chimney," Georgina said softly.

As a finishing touch, George put a small plate on top of the fireplace with a mince pie on it. Next to the mince pie was a large carrot and a small glass of dark red-coloured sherry.

"And the mince pie and sherry are ready for Santa!" George chirped, bouncing in his seat. "And so is the carrot for the reindeer so they can see in the dark when they're flying around the world pulling Santa's sleigh."

"And the stockings are hung by the chimney with care!" Georgina added joyfully, with a big Cheshire Cat grin on her face. "Ready for PRESENTS!"

"Good. Everything's ready then," Granny said. She looked over at the tall Grandfather Clock in the corner of the room, ticking loudly.

"My, my, look at the time. Shouldn't you both be in bed by now? You can't be awake when Santa gets here."

"But Granny... what if he doesn't come?" George muttered in a small, worried voice, his eyes wide.

"He will come. He always comes. That was the agreement," Granny assured him.

"Agreement?" wondered George.

"Yes," Granny explained. "Santa Claus agreed with Mumble that he would come every year to visit all the children and bring presents for them. And every year he's done just that, just as he promised."

"Granny, I'm confused," Georgina said with one
eyebrow raised. "What agreement? And who's Mumble?"

Granny smiled. "Children, come and sit by my feet. I
want to tell you a story...."

George and Georgina came to sit with their legs crossed
at the foot of Granny's armchair. Georgina had her teddy bear,
Mr Snuggles, in her lap and George had his teddy bear, Mrs
Snuggles, in his. Dipstick came and sat in between the two
children. He was panting with excitement, but he calmed down
a little and looked at Granny with thoughtful eyes. He seemed
to be interested in what Granny had to say. He dropped his
squeaky ball and lay down with his paws set together. And
then Granny began her story...

Chapter Two
Murmur and the Elf

It was a long, long time ago in a village called East Pudding, which was next to a vast area of woodland called Pudding Woods. It was a cold, cold night. In fact, it was Christmas Eve and everyone in the village was getting ready for the big day.

Mrs Carter was making iced cookies and Mr Bottletopper was making mince pies and Christmas pudding.

Mr and Mrs Dumples were setting their table for Christmas dinner with a pretty tablecloth, fairy-patterned place mats and Christmas crackers.

Mr Ribbet was decorating the giant Christmas tree in the village square with fairy lights, tinsel and shining baubles.

The baubles were reflecting the snowflakes that had started to fall across the village, covering it in snow in time for the big day.

Miss Bella-Swiss was hanging mistletoe above her front door, and everyone else in East Pudding was wrapping their Christmas presents and putting them under their Christmas trees.

15

But there was
one person who
was not happy about
the arrival of Christmas.

Not happy at all.

The evil witch, Murmur.

Murmur hated Christmas. She hated
how it had started and she hated that it
kept on happening every year, even though
she always did everything she could to try and
stop it. Murmur lived in a dark, stone castle on
the other side of Pudding Woods. A castle that was
surrounded by evil-looking trees. She lived there with
her servants. Horrible goblins who she called her 'elves'.

They were frightening creatures with big, pointy ears and pointy noses, who walked around on all fours and looked like giant spiders.

But the elves weren't as frightening as Murmur herself. The witch was thin and eerily beautiful, with sharp black hair. Her silky, thick black cloak rippled like a wind-blown lake as she walked.

But she always kept parts of herself hidden. You could only see one of her arms for starters. She kept the other one shrouded in the folds of her cloak. Another thing she kept hidden under her cloak was... her tail.

Yes, Murmur had a tail. One that looked just like that of a giant scorpion. You see, in order to spread her evil, Murmur would use her tail to sting people and fill them with her evil like a poison. Her tail would creep out from beneath her cloak, rise and arch over her body and then the giant stinger would come plunging down. And that would be it. The evil would spread through you like a disease.

This is what happened to her elves. They used to be people, you see. Just normal people. But Murmur got to them. Her scorpion tail came out and stung them, filling them with her evil, transforming them into twisted, deformed monsters.

Murmur was not only frightening. She was dangerous. And now that Christmas had come again, Murmur was having her worst bad mood all year, which made her... deadly.

"I'm sick of all this," Murmur snapped at one of her servant elves as she sat on her throne. She was listening to the tiny sound of Christmas Eve carol-singing by the villagers of East Pudding, carried on the wind all the way to her castle.

"I'm sick of this Christmas thing they do every year," she grumbled. "I try and stop it every time, but it just keeps coming. I've had enough. I don't want to hear carols anymore. I don't want to see Christmas lights spilling into the trees anymore. I don't want to hear all this joy and laughter anymore. The sound of generosity, of kindness. It's all nonsense."

"What do you want me to do, Mistress?" the evil elf croaked, whose name was Atnas, in a horrible grating voice that sounded like fingernails scratching a tree.

"I want you to go to East Pudding, Atnas," Murmur said in a deep, commanding voice. "I want you to take the Toe-Eaters with you and leave some in every single house. I want Christmas to be destroyed, once and for all."

"Of course, Mistress," said Atnas obediently. "It will be done."

So Atnas set off into the night.

Chapter Three
Atnas, the Christmas Monster

By the time Atnas reached East Pudding, all the villagers were asleep and dreaming of eating roast turkey and opening presents. All the houses were unlit and quiet inside.

Everything was ready for Christmas Day. The fairy lights on the big village Christmas tree had gone out and would not be turned on again until Christmas Day evening. Now only silver moonlight shone across the houses, making the falling snowflakes glisten like gems. It was the perfect time for the evil elf to set traps for all the children of the village.

Atnas had taken with him to East Pudding a large green sack. Inside the sack were hundreds of little creatures called Toe-Eaters. Now the Toe-Eaters were nasty little things. They were round like balls with mouldy-looking skin, one horrible staring eye, a mouth full of sharp teeth and bat-like ears. They were called the Toe-Eaters because they would lurk in the shadows and attack anybody who walked by near them by chewing off their toes.

But they hadn't always been like this. In fact they did not used to be alive at all.

The Toe-Eaters used to be oranges. Before Murmur came along, the orange trees in the Orange Grove That Was had lots of juicy oranges which the people in East Pudding would come and pick to make orange juice, marmalade and all sorts of delicious foods.

However, in a particularly foul temper one day, Murmur decided to turn them into little monsters. She went to each orange tree in turn and used her stinger to pierce them and fill them with her evil. When she did this, a horrible black substance spread through each tree, turning them thin, grey and crooked. The leaves crumbled into dust and, finally, the oranges hanging from the branches transformed into the Toe-Eaters.

Atnas, with his green sack of Toe-Eaters, started moving through the village, his gangly hands making spider-shaped prints in the thick snow. He didn't want to wake anyone up. If he did, Murmur's plan might fail. He took very light steps, light as a bubble. He had to be as quiet as a shadow.

What Atnas hadn't figured out was how he was going to get inside the houses to deposit the Toe-Eaters. All of the villagers had locked their front doors. All their windows were shut and locked too.

But gradually, like Murmur's poison spreads through her victims, an evil idea began to unfurl in Atnas' mind. Of course! thought Atnas as he looked around at all of the houses.

They all had chimneys.

Atnas could climb up the walls of each house onto the roof and then squeeze down the chimney. Perfect!

So he did.

He began at the first house on Tulip Avenue and climbed up the side of the house with his green sack of Toe-Eaters, like a giant spider crawling up the wall. He scrambled onto the snow-covered roof and slipped quietly down the chimney. He wriggled and squirmed down the black, sooty walls of the flue and landed in the fireplace on a heap of warm logs.

He crept out and looked around the living room. A cosy place. The Christmas tree stood majestically with a fairy on top, fairy lights all over the branches and presents wrapped in colourful wrapping paper and ribbons underneath. There were also chocolates wrapped in foil hanging from the branches. Atnas took a chocolate, unwrapped it and ate it. "Yummy," he whispered.

Then he saw lots of pairs of child-sized socks hanging above the fireplace across the mantelpiece. There were blue socks and pink socks so it looked like a little boy and a little girl lived in the house. The socks had been hung there to dry by the children's Mum and Dad.

Perfect, the evil elf thought with a wicked grin. He opened up his green sack. Inside the mouldy-looking Toe-Eaters wiggled and jiggled. They hissed like snakes and snapped their jaws together. Their sharp teeth twinkled. Atnas took out one of the Toe-Eaters and slipped it inside the first sock hanging above the fireplace.

Then he took out another Toe-Eater and dropped it inside the second sock. Then he put a third Toe-Eater inside the third sock. He kept doing this until all the socks were filled.

The children would come down in the morning to put their feet in their clean, dry socks, and then the Toe-Eaters would bite off their toes, one by one. Then Christmas would be ruined! Atnas giggled to himself before creeping back up the chimney and out onto the roof.

Murmur will be so pleased with me, he thought. He went down the chimneys of three more houses. He put Toe-Eaters in all the socks and stockings that were hanging to dry by the chimney.

Then he went to the fifth house in East Pudding. He slithered down the sooty chimney and into the living room. He was just about to start filling the polka-dot-covered socks hanging by the chimney with Toe-Eaters, when suddenly -

"*Aaaahhhh*!!"

Chapter Four
Atnas meets Heather

The shrill scream of a little girl bounced off all the walls of the living room and pounded inside the evil elf's ears like a drum. Atnas spun round. In the doorway to the living room, there stood a shocked little girl called Heather with shoulder-length brown hair and lots of freckles, wearing a pink nightie. She had just come downstairs to get a glass of milk and found a monster in her house.

"Who are you?!!" Heather gasped, holding her hand over her mouth.

"I'm the one who is going to have to eat you to stop you waking up the village with that foghorn voice of yours," hissed Atnas in his scratchy voice.

"Eat me?!" cried Heather with alarm. "You can't eat me!"

"Why not?"

"Because... because I'm going to be a ballerina! Please don't eat me! I want to be the best ballerina in the village! I can't do that if you eat me!"

Heather had always wanted to dance and she loved ballet. She hadn't had a chance to become a ballerina yet, because her Mum and Dad couldn't afford to buy her a pair of ballet slippers. They were quite expensive, so they were saving their pennies to buy her a pair.

But Atnas didn't care about Heather wanting to be a ballerina. Of course he didn't. He was evil, just like Murmur.

He started to walk towards her. Heather backed away.

"Please! I'll be quiet!" Heather said, in a mouse's whisper. "Please!!"

Atnas continued to step towards her. The moonlight was lighting up his horrible, rotten-looking teeth. He licked his lips with a long, slimy, green tongue.

"P-p-p-please... Who...who are you?" Heather squeaked, her heart pounding. She was breathing heavily.

"I am..." Atnas whispered. "I am...."

Suddenly Atnas's already twisted face twisted a little more. He was thinking about something. He looked down at his belly, which he rubbed with his bony hand. His belly made a grumbling sound.

"I am.... getting hungry." Atnas finally finished his sentence.

"Noooo!" screamed Heather. "Please!"

Atnas licked his horrible lips once more. He stepped closer.....

"Stop!" Heather had an idea! "If you're hungry," she said, "there are mince pies in the kitchen, left over from earlier! Have some of those! They'll be much tastier than me!"

"Mince pies?" There was excitement in Atnas' voice. His mouth started to produce lots of squelchy spit.

"Yes! I'll show you!" shouted Heather gleefully.

Heather trotted into the kitchen and Atnas followed. On the work surface were some mince pies and a half-finished glass of sherry which her Mum had left out.

Atnas grabbed several of the mince pies, tossed them in his mouth and swallowed all of them at once.

"You gannet!" giggled Heather.

Then Atnas picked up the glass of sherry and washed the sticky, spicy mince pies down with that. "Mmmmm," gurgled Atnas, wiping his mouth of sugar and crumbs and grinning.

And then something happened. Atnas stopped smiling and his face twisted again. He was thinking about something. And this time it wasn't his belly.

He was remembering something. He remembered eating mince pies and sherry before. But how? And then he had a flash. It was like a flash of light before his eyes and suddenly he could see an image of himself. He could see himself a long time ago and he looked completely different.

No longer did he look like an elf. He had normal ears, a normal face and his arms and legs were no longer like a spider's legs. He looked like a person. He was remembering being with his friends, drinking sherry and eating mince pies. They were his favourite snack.

Or they used to be. Before Murmur came and took it all away. Took away his friends, his mince pies and his sherry. And turned him into an elf.

"What?" asked Heather, noticing that something strange had happened to the elf. "What's wrong?!"

Then a huge, deep, booming voice announced....

"He's remembering. He's remembering that he wasn't always evil."

Heather and Atnas spun around. Standing in the doorway to the kitchen was a very tall man in a purple cloak, with a pointed beard.

"Don't mind me," the man twinkled. "I just let myself in through the back door. Hope you don't mind. Ooooo! Any mince pies left?"

Chapter Five
The Good Wizard Arrives

"Mumble!" cried Heather happily. "It's you!"

The man who had just appeared in Heather's house was the good wizard, Mumble. Mumble lived in the castle on the edge of East Pudding and looked after the village. And he LOVED Christmas.

"Hello Heather," said Mumble warmly. He had a voice like a king.

He then turned to Atnas, frowned, put his hands on his hips and scolded, "Soooo, Mr Funny-Spider-Elf-Thing-With-A-Weird-Face. You're the one who's been stealing all the rabbits from my garden!"

"Huh?" said Atnas blankly. "No, I haven't!"

"Oh no, wait," Mumble said. "I do apologise. My train of thought has derailed."

The confused wizard took a little notebook out from inside his majestic cloak and flicked through it. Heather peered at the notebook, but all she could see were strange symbols, funny doodles and a fair few tea stains, so it was anyone's guess how Mumble could make sense of it.

"You're right!" Mumble blurted loudly. "Sorry, wrong person, wrong crime. You're Christmas-ruining, aren't you, not rabbit-stealing. Do excuse me."

"That's all right," said Atnas, bewildered.

"So where was I? Ah, yes. Soooo, Mr Funny-Spider-Elf-Thing-With-A-Weird-Face, you're the one who's been trying to ruin Christmas by putting Toe-Eaters in people's stockings!"

"Urm, I don't know what you're talking about," Atnas muttered innocently, but looking very guilty.

"Tell me the truth! Or I'll make you eat liquorice!" Mumble shouted like a teacher at a naughty pupil.

"OKAY!!" Atnas admitted. "It was me! I did it!" You see, liquorice was the most disgusting thing in the world to an elf. Mumble shook his head disapprovingly.

"What are you going to do to me?" Atnas asked in a frightened whimper.

"Well, I'll tell you what I'm going to do," Mumble barked sternly. Then he paused for about a minute.

"Okay..." said Atnas, waiting. "What?"

"What?" said Mumble blankly.

"I said, what are you going to do to me?" Atnas repeated.

"Yes, I heard you. I'm about to tell you."

Mumble screwed up his face and looked up as if he was thinking. His train of thought had derailed again.

"Er... Mumble," Heather prompted him.

"Oh yes!" yelped Mumble suddenly. "Sorry, allow me to reshuffle my thinking cogs. What did you say again?"

"I SAID, what are you going to do to me?" Atnas repeated for the second time, becoming frustrated.

"Well, I'll tell you what I'm going to do. What I'm going to do is..." Mumble leaned close to Atnas's face. The elf's heart was pounding like a bull running across a field. "... ask you a question," Mumble finished with a flourish.

Atnas sighed with relief. He really thought he was a goner. He swallowed hard.

"And my question is, why are you still listening to Murmur?" Mumble said.

"Murmur is my ruler," explained Atnas. "She is the Mistress of Darkness. Queen of all Evil. Lady of the Shadows."

"Yes, yes, yes, I know all that. She does love her titles, that Murmur. But you've just started to remember your life before her, haven't you? When you used to be a human being. And do you remember being... happy?"

"Happy...." Atnas pondered this for a second. Happy - that was a feeling he had forgotten all about until now.

"Yes," he puffed, his mouth stretching into a new smile. This one was not a smirk of evil. It was a smile of happiness. Suddenly there was a warm feeling running through him which felt very unusual.

"Yes, I remember being happy," Atnas whispered.

"Murmur made you forget what that means," Mumble explained. "She turned you into a monster. A monster who doesn't care about others."

"But Murmur says that you shouldn't care about others. She says you should always put yourself first and look after number one. Don't ever be generous or kind to other people. Be selfish. That's how you become strong and powerful. And strength and power is what matters. It's how you stay happy and secure."

"And alone," Mumble added.

"Being alone is good, Murmur says. She says that if you look after yourself and don't rely on anyone else, there's no one to disappoint you."

"And there's no one to cuddle you when you're sad either. Or make you happy. Or make you laugh. Look at you now. You're alone and you're unhappy. You've forgotten what it means to be happy, because Murmur has made you stop caring about others. Now you have no friends. No family. No one who cares about *you*. Because Murmur surely doesn't."

"Because she only cares about herself," Atnas said bitterly. He was finally realizing.

"Exactly," Mumble agreed, nodding. "And that's why *she* has no friends."

"I'm starting to remember, Mumble," Atnas gasped, his voice filled with awe. "I'm starting to remember who I used to be. I'm starting to...."

36

Suddenly something happened.
Atnas' body started to change. His thin,
twig-like arms and legs became fatter and
his twisted body straightened.

His large pointed ears shrunk and
started to become round again.
And then hair began to grow on
top of his head.

He was no longer an elf.
He was a man again.

Chapter Six
A Happy Man Returns

"That's Murmur's evil," said Mumble, explaining what had happened. "It's all left your body."

"Wow!" exclaimed Atnas, with a new human voice instead of a low, throaty growl. He wore an excited grin and his eyes were as wide as an owl's as he looked at his newly restored hands and feet.

"Let's find you some warm clothes, shall we?" Mumble suggested.

He poked his head inside his cloak, looking in the inside pockets. He peered in the pockets on the left side of his cloak, then poked in the ones on the right side.

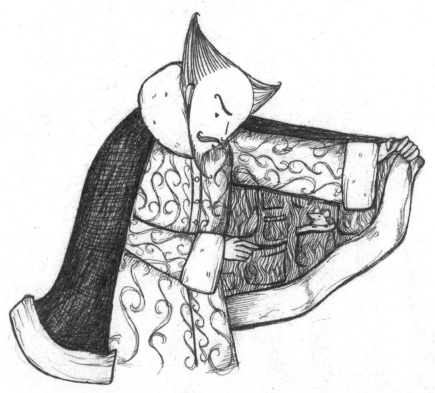

Atnas raised his eyebrow, confused by what Mumble was doing. Suddenly, out of an improbably small pocket, Mumble produced a huge coat with big black buttons, white fluffy fur down the middle and on the cuffs, and a black leather belt. How Mumble had managed to fit it inside his own cloak was a mystery.

"Here. Put this on," said Mumble. Atnas wrapped himself in the big red coat and fastened the buttons.

Then Mumble pulled out a red, white-fur-trimmed hat with a white fluffy bobble on the end.

"And definitely this," said Mumble, popping the hat onto Atnas' head.

Mumble reached into his magical pocket one last time and pulled out a pair of baggy, white-cuffed red trousers, along with a pair of big, black, shiny boots.

"And of course these," Mumble said finally, presenting the boots and trousers to Atnas.

"What is all this?" asked Atnas.

"Oh, just an old outfit of mine," Mumble replied. "I went off the colour red. I discovered purple, you see. But I think it suits you."

Atnas pulled on the trousers and the boots. He liked how the outfit felt against his restored human skin. Warm and snuggly. Perfect for a winter's night.

Then Atnas noticed Heather. She had sat down at the kitchen table while he and Mumble were talking and had fallen asleep with her head resting on her arms. It was the middle of the night after all, and children need their sleep.

"What shall I do now, Mumble?" asked Atnas, whispering so he wouldn't wake Heather up.

"Well, I don't think you should eat Heather," said Mumble matter-of-factly, stroking his beard.

"I know that!" Atnas laughed.

"D'you know what I think you should do instead? I'll tell you what I think you should do."

"Okay... What?" replied Atnas, preparing for another of Mumble's confused rambles.

"I'm about to tell you."

Mumble screwed up his face and looked up again dreamily.

"Mr Jellybum!!" Mumble then cried excitedly. "He's the rabbit-stealer! Remind me, I need to go and see him next."

"Okay, sure," Atnas muttered indifferently. "What were you about to tell me?"

"What? When?"

"Just now! About what you think I should do instead of eating Heather!"

"Oh, yes! Sorry, I need to un-boggle my brain..."

There was another pause. Atnas tapped his foot with frustration. This wizard could try anyone's patience!

"I remember! Yes, this is what I think you should do," Mumble declared finally. "I think you should leave Heather a present. Christmas is all about sharing and giving."

"I haven't got any presents to give," Atnas said sadly. "I've only got Toe-Eaters. Speaking of which...."

Atnas remembered that he had left his green sack of Toe-Eaters on the floor in the living room.

"Oh no!" he cried when he saw one of the Toe-Eaters bobbing into the kitchen like a tennis ball. Well, a tennis ball with an eye.

With its one scary eye wide and staring, and slobber dribbling from the corners of its mouth, the Toe-Eater bobbed along the white tiles on the kitchen floor towards Heather, who was still asleep at the kitchen table.

"Oh no!" shrieked Atnas. "Heather's feet! It's going for her toes!"

Heather's legs had flopped to one side underneath the table and her bare feet were on display - much to the excitement of the Toe-Eater that was running towards them. Yummy! thought the Toe-Eater. Yummy toes - all for me!

But before the Toe-Eater could reach her feet and bite off her toes, Mumble reached inside his purple coat and pulled out his white magic wand. He pointed it at the Toe-Eater and shouted, "Spagalogagog!"

And then - pop!

There was a small flash of yellow light, a little puff of smoke and - a moment later - the Toe-Eater had turned into a little box. A little box with a surprise gift inside it. A little box wrapped in pink paper with flowers on it, and a red ribbon tied around it into a bow.

The Toe-Eater had turned into a Christmas present. Meanwhile Heather was still fast asleep and hadn't noticed a thing.

"Now you have a present for Heather," said Mumble with a grin, picking the present up off the floor and handing it to Atnas.

"But what about...?" said Atnas. He ran past Mumble to the doorway that led from the kitchen into the living room. "Oh no!" he yelled.

He saw his green sack of Toe-Eaters lying by the Christmas tree. The sack was open and the Toe-Eaters were all bobbing out of it, bouncing across the carpet looking for toes.

When they saw Atnas in the doorway, they looked up with their eerie solitary eyes and stared. Then they looked down. Their mouths stretched into toothy grins when they noticed Heather's feet through the doorway to the kitchen.

Yummy toes! they all thought. They didn't lick their lips because they didn't have any lips. So they just licked their whole faces instead.

But even though Mumble's brain was a bit slow, his body was as quick as a cat. He ran up behind Atnas, pointed his wand at the cluster of Toe-Eaters and shouted, "Spagalogagog! Fuzzynipperswitch!" (The 'fuzzynipperswitch' was to make the spell work on all the Toe-Eaters at once, you see).

And then.... pop!

One by one, with flashes of light and puffs of smoke, the Toe-Eaters turned into Christmas presents. All with different coloured wrapping paper and different coloured bows.

44

Pop!

Pop!

Pop!

Mumble and Atnas both sighed with relief, catching their breath. Heather's house was safe again.

"D'you know what I think you should do now?" Mumble whispered softly.

"I've got an inkling..." said Atnas.

"I think you should take these presents to all the houses in East Pudding and put one in each sock or stocking you see hanging to dry. Rather than getting nasty surprises by putting their feet in socks filled with Toe-Eaters, the children will get nice surprises instead."

"Now that IS a good idea. I like it," smiled Atnas.

Atnas gathered up the presents, placed them inside the green sack, and flung the sack over his shoulder. He still had Heather's present in his hand so he walked towards the fireplace and dropped the present into one of her polka-dot-covered socks that was hanging from the mantelpiece.

He smiled again when he looked back at Heather in the kitchen. He could see her just around the frame of the doorway, still sitting at the table fast asleep.

She'll be so surprised when she wakes up on Christmas morning! Atnas thought gleefully.

He was just about to climb into the fireplace and go back up the chimney when Mumble stopped him.

"Wait," Mumble commanded. "Mr Used-To-Be-A-Funny-Spider-Elf-Thing-With-A-Weird-Face. What is your real name?"

Atnas thought about this for a moment. Then he said, "I don't... I don't remember my name. I don't remember what I was called before Murmur turned me into an evil elf. I only remember the name she gave me."

"And what name was that?" Mumble asked.

"Atnas. Atnas Sualc."

"Atnas Sualc? Mmmmm. Okay..... Oh! I have an idea!" Mumble said eagerly.

"What's that?"

"Well, you've turned your life around tonight. So you should turn your name around too. Mmmmm. So 'Atnas' backwards is... urm... bear with me. Urm, Atnas.... That's urm... hmm... that's...."

Mumble kept on speaking, but his voice got quieter and Atnas could hardly hear what Mumble was saying. Mumble had started to - mumble!

"Right, that's errrr..." Mumble continued unsurely. "Yes, that's errrr. Sorry, let me un-fog my noggin... I was never any good at Maths."

"Maths?" said Atnas with a confused look.

"No, not Maths! That's numbers. I mean... English! I was never any good at English! Spelling, I mean. My spelling's not great. Urrrm..."

There was a long pause as Mumble continued to get his brain into gear.

Then Atnas noticed in the corner of the living room a small heap of Heather's toys, including a set of painted, wooden building blocks with letters on them.

"There. Look. Maybe these will help," suggested Atnas, walking over to the building blocks, crouching down and starting to rearrange them.

He laid out in front of him on the carpet a row of ten

building blocks spelling out his first name, "A T N A S", and then his second name, "S U A L C". Mumble strode over to Atnas, and with a flourish of his wand, switched the blocks around, so that each word was back to front.

"Ah yes," Mumble then announced proudly. "ATNAS backwards is SANTA and SUALC backwards is CLAUS!"

Chapter Seven
Santa Claus is Born

"So that's my new name?"Atnas asked Mumble. "Santa Claus?"

"Yes! Santa Claus! Wonderful! Perfect!" cried Mumble joyfully, starting to clap his hands together, giving himself a round of applause for being so clever.

"I kinda like it," muttered Santa with a grin.

"Well, you better hurry and deliver those presents, Santa Claus! It won't be Christmas Eve forever!"

So Santa Claus climbed up Heather's chimney back onto the snow-covered roof. He paid visits to all the houses in East Pudding and, instead of putting Toe-Eaters inside children's socks and stockings to bite off the children's toes, he put presents inside them instead.

Meanwhile, Mumble sneaked inside the four houses that Santa had already been in, when he was still an evil elf. He waved his magic wand over the socks which contained wriggling Toe-Eaters and turned each Toe-Eater into a little Christmas present. He did this until all the Toe-Eaters were gone and every house in East Pudding was safe again.

Some time later, Mumble and Santa met again in the village square. The snow was still falling like sugar lumps. The village looked so pretty and quiet.

"I like doing this," Santa grinned. "The children are going to be so surprised and happy when they find secret

presents in their stockings tomorrow morning! I think I want to do this every year."

"Good idea," said Mumble, placing his hand on Santa's shoulder. "I think you should do that too. It will make Christmas even more special. And if you do that, I will make sure that every family leaves a mince pie and a sherry out for you when you visit their house. Because I know they're your favourite."

"Agreed!" cried Santa happily. "But a mince pie and sherry in every house? I'll get very fat!"

"Just make sure you do lots of exercise," Mumble advised. "Because if you get too fat, you won't fit down people's chimneys!" Mumble laughed. Santa laughed too.

But there was someone
on the other side of Pudding
Woods who wasn't laughing.

She wasn't even smiling.

Murmur.

She was in her castle looking into a cauldron of bubbling, dark red liquid. Could've been blood. Who knows? She was scowling, biting her lip and getting angrier and angrier as she watched what the cauldron was showing her.

In the red liquid she could see an image of her former servant, Atnas, now Santa, climbing down chimneys in East Pudding and leaving presents inside children's stockings.

She was enraged. Steam was coming out of her ears. Her face was red like a beetroot. She was grinding her fingernails into her palm till blood started trickling to the floor.

"Mumble has interfered with my plans for the last time," Murmur whispered firmly.

"What are you going to do, Mistress?" growled one of her elves.

"Well, Atnas has proved that if you want something done around here, you have to do it yourself!" Murmur shouted. "So I'm going to East Pudding right now to finish Atnas' job!"

Chapter Eight
Murmur's Fury

The snow outside Murmur's castle was thick, so Murmur swept into the south tower of the castle to get her sleigh.

Meanwhile she got the elves to round up her reindeer, who were evil-looking, four-legged creatures with twisted bodies, crooked legs, colossal antlers and huge mouths that were full of sharp teeth.

Murmur's reindeer lived in the shadows of the trees in Pudding Woods and would pounce on and trample anyone who might be brave enough to pass through the shadows.

Of course, they too didn't used to be like that. Reindeer used to be quite nice. Just like the Toe-Eaters used to be simple oranges. But Murmur turned all the reindeer into monsters by stinging them with her tail and filling their blood with evil.

Now the reindeer were another reason the people of East Pudding stayed out of the woods.

Murmur also gathered up a horde of Toe-Eaters and piled them into her sleigh. They all wriggled and jiggled and made slurping sounds, their solitary eyes blinking.

Her elves brought the reindeer to her as she was setting up her sleigh outside the castle and getting ready to go. The reindeer made spitting and hissing noises.

One of the reindeer charged at one of the elves and trampled on him till he was dead. Then another reindeer did the same to another elf.

"Recnad! Neztilb!" Murmur shouted angrily at the two reindeer responsible. "Do NOT kill my elves! Or I won't let you pull my sleigh and you won't get any carrots!"

Recnad and Neztilb immediately decided to behave. Temoc and Recnarp giggled.

Murmur buckled reins to each of the reindeer and fastened them to her sleigh so that the reindeer would pull the sleigh. Then she got into it. She glanced behind to check on the Toe-Eaters, who were all squirming and slurping in the back of the sleigh.

She raised her magic wand, which unlike Mumble's, looked like a horrible, twisted tree root. A thin strip of lightning shot out of the end of the magic wand and struck the lead reindeer on the bottom. The reindeer was startled, made a horrible screeching sound and suddenly moved forwards.

Or rather, it tried to.

The snow was so thick that all the reindeer were ankle-deep in it. They couldn't move their hooves through the snow.

Murmur used another bolt of lightning to try and encourage the reindeer, but it was no use. They weren't going anywhere. They were stuck. And the snow was still coming down fast and heavy.

"Fine," Murmur hissed, trying to stay calm but getting more and more infuriated. "If we can't make it on foot, we'll have to try... on air!"

All the reindeer craned their necks around to look at Murmur with puzzled expressions.

On air?

Murmur raised her wand again and this time, instead of lightning, a huge puff of what looked like powdery shards of broken glass came out of the end. The dust engulfed the reindeer in a cloud and each of them started to choke.

A moment later the dust had settled and the reindeer were all looking at each other. They had no idea what had just happened.

Then Murmur shot another thin strip of lightning out of her wand at the lead reindeer's bottom. The reindeer was startled, gave a piercing screech and suddenly started flying!

One by one, each of the reindeer rose off the ground, as if a mysterious force was lifting them into the air. They didn't know how but suddenly they were floating on the air, drifting up into the trees. They started kicking their legs as if they were galloping and they flew forwards.

They pulled Murmur's sleigh up and out of the trees.

She then shouted, "Take me to East Pudding at once!", and the reindeer started flying in the direction of the village.

Behind Murmur, the Toe-Eaters were licking their faces and working up big appetites for toes. As she sat in her sleigh, Murmur could feel her anger boiling and bubbling inside her. For years she had been trying to get rid of Christmas. For years Mumble and the people of East Pudding had got in her way. She had finally had enough.

"But I mustn't let my anger get the better of me," Murmur told herself. "I must keep my temper in check. Otherwise... I might just go mad."

As she said this, East Pudding came into view in the distance. Right! Murmur thought. This is it!

Chapter Nine
The Last Battle

Santa and Mumble were still standing in the village square when the purple wizard noticed in the corner of his eye Murmur's dark sleigh, pulled by nine reindeer, crossing the sky and coming towards them. He turned and whispered, as if he had been waiting for her arrival, "Here she comes."

As she started passing over the houses, Murmur turned around in her sleigh and grabbed a pile of Toe-Eaters. Then she tossed them overboard. The Toe-Eaters plunged towards the ground, ready to start attacking any feet that came near them, including those of Mumble and Santa.

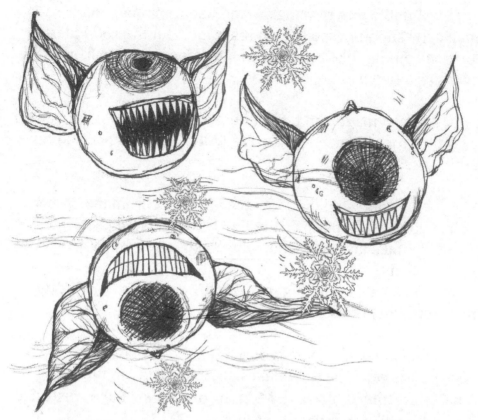

Mumble raised his wand quickly. "Spagalogagog! Fuzzynipperswitch!" he bellowed. Before the Toe-Eaters reached the ground, lots of popping sounds pierced the night air and they turned into Christmas presents. The presents landed all around in the soft snow. "Ha! Gotcha!" shouted Mumble triumphantly.

Murmur threw more Toe-Eaters at the village. As nimble as he was, Mumble couldn't move fast enough to catch them all. There were too many and Mumble was getting old.

Some of them landed in people's chimneys and found their way into living rooms and kitchens. Lots of them landed in the streets and in the square and started bobbing and wriggling towards Santa and Mumble.

Mumble was twirling around like a spinning top, manically shooting spells with his wand. But the Toe-Eaters kept on coming, like a shower of hailstones with teeth, as Murmur threw them out of her sleigh.

"This village will be infested with Toe-Eaters!" screamed Murmur from the sky. "Christmas will be ruined once and for all!"

"Murmur, stop this!" shouted Mumble from the ground. "Must you always be so annoying? Why can't we just have a nice cup of tea and talk about what's bothering you?"

"YOU are bothering me! And I'm about to put a stop to it!" Murmur shrieked in reply.

Suddenly, the snow falling from the sky started to become heavier. The snowflakes got fatter and multiplied, quickly creating a blizzard. Millions of fat snowflakes rushed at Murmur and her reindeer's faces.

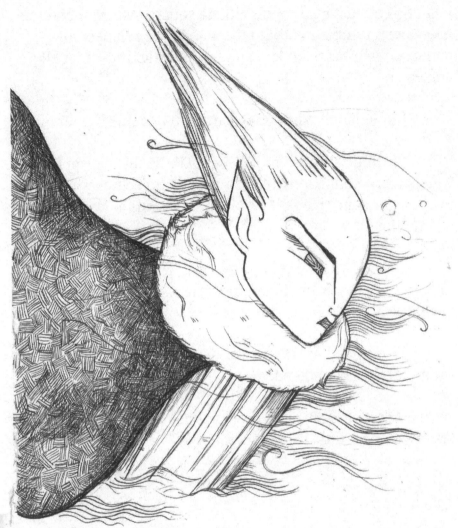

"Nooo!" screamed Murmur. "Stop! I can't see!" Soon
Murmur couldn't see anything ahead of her sleigh. There was
just too much snow. She couldn't see where she was going and
neither could her reindeer. Mumble, smiling down below and
still zapping the Toe-Eaters with his wand, saw what was about
to happen.

Murmur's sleigh grazed one of the trees in East Pudding,
which caused it to swerve towards the ground. The reindeer
were scrambling on the air, but they were blinded by the snow.
They didn't know which way was up. The sleigh crashed in the

High Street, just next to the village square. Murmur and the Toe-Eaters tumbled out into the snow. The reindeer all collapsed in a heap, antlers and hooves sticking out at all angles.

Immediately, the snow started to become lighter again.

Murmur climbed to her feet. All the muscles in her face were stretched in a look of fury. She clutched her wand tight in her right hand. Her silky cloak flapped in the wind. She was not at all happy now.

"Hello, Murmur," Mumble said chummily. "Wow, you look like you've been on the pies. Getting a bit of a belly there, I see!"

This tipped Murmur over the edge. "You will DIE, Mumble!" she thundered.

"Oh, that's boring. How long have we been doing this? Can't you be a little more imaginative?"

"All right then..." Murmur snarled. "How is this for imaginative?"

Suddenly Murmur dropped down onto all fours. Her huge scorpion tail burst out from beneath her cloak, actually throwing her cloak off her body and into the snow, revealing more of the hideous body she kept hidden beneath.

Actually, Murmur didn't just have a scorpion tail. She was half-scorpion. The arm that she kept hidden was in fact a scorpion pincer. And instead of normal human legs, she had eight, sharp, pointy scorpion legs. She scuttled towards Mumble, scattering cobbles in her wake.

"Now what do you have to say, Mumble?" Murmur taunted as she came closer and closer to Mumble's face.

"All I have to say to you is...." Mumble whispered, with a very serious look on his face, "I think you need to moisturise. You're getting frown lines."

"Aaaarrrrggghhh!!!" Murmur suddenly shrieked, lunging at Mumble. Her scorpion sting plunged towards his face.

"Mumble, nooo!" Santa cried, running towards the purple wizard.

Santa ran in front of Mumble just as Murmur's huge tail came plunging down.

And then Murmur stung Santa on the neck.

Santa collapsed. A horrible black substance started to spread from his neck across his face. His body started to twist and become thin and spindly, and his ears started to grow and become pointy.

He was turning back into an evil elf.

"Right," said Mumble sternly. "Murmur, that's it. I've tried to be nice. Now I'm going to get... less nice."

Mumble raised his wand. Sparks and surges fizzled at its tip. He pointed it at the huge half-scorpion monster and a powerful blue bolt of lightning shot out of the wand towards her. The lightning flung Murmur across the village square into the huge village Christmas tree, which then toppled and fell right on top of her.

For a moment everything was still.

But then, underneath the tree, sparks hissed and spat. Little bolts of lightning cracked through the branches. The spot underneath the tree where Murmur had landed began to glow a bright yellow.

Suddenly the Christmas tree was tossed like a toy across

the village and landed in a heap
in Miss Bella-Swiss' garden.

Mumble squinted into the
blinding light that was coming
from Murmur. He couldn't see her
anymore.

He couldn't see her
hideous scorpion body.

He could just see a
huge ball of light,
with streaks of
lightning shooting
out of it every
second.

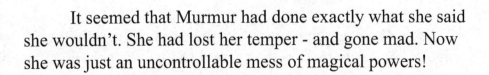

It seemed that Murmur had done exactly what she said
she wouldn't. She had lost her temper - and gone mad. Now
she was just an uncontrollable mess of magical powers!

"Look what you've done to me, Mumble!" Murmur
screamed. "Now I've lost my temper!"

Bolts of lightning were shooting out of Murmur in every
direction. Some bolts struck the trees, lighting up the sky in

jagged flashes. Some of them bounced off the houses, flinging tiles off the roofs and snapping bricks off the chimneys. And some of them struck the ground.

"Stoooop!!" screamed Mumble in a panic, realizing what was about to happen. "Murmur!! You're going to cause... You're going to cause an...!"

Suddenly one of the bolts of lightning hit the ground so hard that it cracked. A huge crack ripped across all of East Pudding, right through the village square. The lightning fizzed and crackled back and forth, widening the crack.

"...Earthquake!!!" Mumble shrieked.

People in their houses could hear the commotion outside and many started to wake up. Mums and Dads told their children to stay in bed while they went to their windows to look outside at what was happening.

They saw the huge gorge in the ground that Murmur's lightning storm had created. It was still getting wider and wider until the village had literally been split in half.

"Mumble, I've had ENOUGH!!!" Murmur screamed hysterically. "I've had enough of yooooou!!!"

While she was screaming, Murmur was stood right on the edge of the gaping rift in the ground she had just created. Inside the crack there was nothing but darkness. It was a shadowy chasm that just went on and on and on.

Suddenly, a section of rocks crumbled at the edge of the gorge, just beneath several of Murmur's scorpion legs. She lost her balance and toppled over the edge.

With a spine-tingling scream that echoed through East Pudding, Pudding Woods and beyond, Murmur plunged down and down into the crack. She looked like a ball of fire that was shrinking as the darkness swallowed her. Her echoing scream faded to a tiny whistle. A moment later, there was nothing. Murmur was gone forever. Killed by her own bad temper.

Mumble looked into the gorge. For a moment he looked troubled, almost sad. Then he muttered bitterly, "At last East Pudding is free of you."

Mumble pointed his wand at the huge crack that went right across the village. Suddenly, with a deafening rasp like hundreds of rocks grinding together, the crack began to close. The two sides of the village came together again.

And then something started happening to the reindeer, who were still lying in a heap by Murmur's sleigh, snarling and grunting. Their crooked legs and twisted bodies straightened out. Their sharp teeth shrunk and their tails became fluffy. Their fur became softer. They weren't scary anymore. In fact, they looked quite cuddly.

Now that Murmur was dead, her evil had left the reindeer. They had turned back into the nice and friendly creatures they used to be. The same thing happened to the Toe-Eaters that Mumble hadn't managed to turn into Christmas presents, including the ones that Murmur had dropped into people's chimneys. They all turned back into harmless oranges.

And of course, Santa, who Murmur had briefly turned back into an evil elf by stinging him, became human once more.

A few villagers who had been woken up by all the commotion were looking out of their windows. Mumble shouted to them, "Everything is under control! All of you go back to sleep! It's not long till Christmas!"

As Mums and Dads put their sleepy children back to bed, one little boy said to his Mum, "Who was that man with the green sack who was dressed in Mumble's old suit?"

"I don't know," his Mum replied. "But I'm sure Mumble will tell us tomorrow. Now go to sleep. It's nearly Christmas."

Meanwhile, Mumble said goodbye to Santa Claus. Santa had gathered up all the presents that used to be Toe-Eaters and put them in his green sack. He was going to keep them for next year.

"What will you do now?" Mumble asked.

"Well, I will take the reindeer with me back to Pudding Woods," Santa said. "And then I will go and free the elves from Murmur's castle. In fact, now that Murmur's dead, they're probably not elves anymore. They've probably turned back into people just like me!"

"Maybe they will help you," Mumble suggested. "Maybe they will help you with your plans to bring presents each Christmas."

"Maybe they will," said Santa, smiling.

He then approached the reindeer. As he did, Mumble called after him, "So you'll be back again next year?"

"Yes, I will," Santa replied surely. "I'll be back again every year."

Santa turned back to the reindeer, who had climbed to their feet with startled expressions on their furry faces. A few moments ago, they were terrifying. Now they were like nervous puppies. They didn't recognise Santa and they were afraid of him. So they started to run away. They were all still attached to Murmur's sleigh so they pulled it along with them.

And suddenly, one by one, they floated up into the air and started flying. It appeared that Murmur's flying spell was permanent! Santa reached out his arm and grabbed hold of one of the runners underneath the sleigh, and was pulled up into the sky with it. He dangled there for a moment, nearly dropping his green sack of presents. Using all of his strength, he climbed up into the sleigh and started steering the frightened reindeer through the sky. He steered them towards Pudding Woods and Murmur's castle to rescue the elves.

And as he passed through the sky over East Pudding, he bellowed loudly, "Merry Christmas to all! And to all a good night! Oh, and Mumble, don't forget about Mr Jellybum! I'm reminding you like you asked!"

"Oh, yes! Rabbit-stealer! Thanks!" Mumble bellowed back, grinning. But Mumble decided to postpone telling Mr Jellybum off for being so naughty and stealing his rabbits to another day. It was nearly Christmas after all.

And so Mumble went home to his castle. As he shut the castle gates and went inside to bed, one last snowflake fell.

Chapter Ten
Surprises on Christmas Morning

When Christmas came the next morning, Heather woke at her kitchen table, thinking about the very strange dream she had had about Mumble and this nasty elf who wanted to eat her.

The tiled kitchen floor was cold against her bare feet. So she went over to where her socks were hanging above the fireplace. She took down her socks and stuffed her left foot into the left sock. Her toes touched something. Something box-like. She tipped the sock upside down and then something fell out.

A little box, wrapped in colourful paper, with a ribbon tied around it into a bow. Just like the presents that her Mum and Dad had put under the Christmas tree.

But who is this present from? thought Heather.

She quickly opened the little present. "Wow!" she cried cheerfully. Inside the box was a pair of ballet slippers. Now Heather could be a ballerina.

Her Mum and Dad were also happy when they found out. Now they could spend the money they had been saving to buy the ballet slippers on something else, which they did. They spent it on making their garden look beautiful when the spring arrived.

Later on Christmas Day, Mumble went to speak to all the confused villagers, who had all found nice surprises in their socks and stockings that morning. And he told them about Santa Claus. He told them what he had done and that he would be back next year to do the same.

And even though Christmas Day was not over yet, all the villagers in East Pudding were excited about next Christmas already.

Meanwhile, Santa Claus made a home out of Murmur's castle. He cleared away the cobwebs, destroyed the sinister stone gargoyles, redecorated the whole place in bright reds and greens, and turned the castle into a giant toy shop, where he and the other former elves set about making more presents for next Christmas.

And when next Christmas came around, Santa Claus returned. He came on Murmur's sleigh, rebuilt and redecorated and made into his own. He came with his flying reindeer. And he came with loads and loads of presents piled into green sacks on the back of the sleigh.

He did it all again as he promised. He went down the chimneys. He left presents in stockings.

And then he flew away again, smiling gleefully at the joy he was bringing.

Only this time, because every house in East Pudding had left a sherry and a mince pie out for him, Santa Claus flew away.... a little fatter than he was the year before!

Chapter Eleven
Time for Bed

"So there you have it, children," said Granny to George and Georgina. "That is how Santa Claus came to be."

The two children were still sat by Granny's feet, listening carefully to the story. Dipstick meanwhile was lying on his back with his legs in the air and his long, wet tongue hanging out of the side of his mouth. He was fast asleep and, given that his legs kept twitching and moving back and forth, he was obviously dreaming about chasing a rabbit or something.

"So... wait," said Georgina. "Santa in the beginning was a monster who put little, one-eyed, mouldy oranges with teeth who like eating people's toes into our stockings?"

"He was once, yes," Granny chuckled. "But he changed, so don't you worry." She smiled warmly at Georgina.

"I might just check my stockings from now on," said Georgina, with a worried look. "Just in case Santa ever decides to go back to his old habits."

Granny laughed.

"And that's why we leave him a sherry and mince pie?" asked George. "Because they're his favourite?"

"Exactly, George. And because they helped Santa remember who he was before Murmur. Plus, they also keep him going on a long night. There's lots more people in the world now, you see. Lots more people than there were then. And Santa's got to deliver to all of them."

"But if Santa's eating mince pies and sherry all across the world, surely he's very, very fat now!" Georgina pointed out.

"Why do you think your Dad had the chimney widened last summer?" said Granny with a smirk.

"Of course!" cried George and Georgina together.

"Now, you two," Granny said firmly. "It's most definitely time for bed. Your Mum and Dad will be very cross with me if I let you stay up any longer. And so will Santa. Now hurry along."

On Granny's order, George took Mrs Snuggles and Georgina took Mr Snuggles and they both marched upstairs to bed.

Georgina was a good girl and went to sleep as soon as her head hit the pillow. She knew that children weren't supposed to be awake when Santa arrived.

76

But George stayed awake a little longer. He knew that he shouldn't, but he was just too excited.

But as time when on, George was getting sleepier.... and sleepier...

He tried to hold on, but he was dropping off...

And by the time the tiny sound of sleigh bells began ringing through the village of Dandiest Pug, George was fast asleep and dreaming about what he would find in his stocking the next morning.

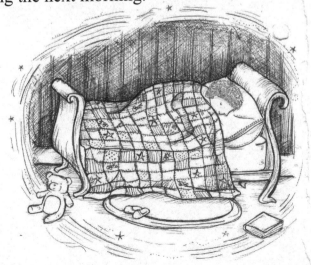

ABOUT THE AUTHOR

Christopher Berry is a lawyer who lives in Farnborough in Hampshire. He works in criminal law and looks after naughty people! He lives with three friends and loves Christmas and Disney movies!

He released another book for children, *The Pendulum Swings*, in April 2011. You can find details about this book on his website, www.berrytimebooks.com, where you can also find poems and short stories – free to read and download! You can also visit his YouTube channel, BerryTimeBooks' Channel, for exciting trailers and poetry films.

It is Christopher's love of Christmas, and in particular the darker side of Christmas in films such as Tim Burton's *The Nightmare Before Christmas*, that inspired him to begin writing *The East Pudding Chronicles*. Christopher has always been interested in the reasons why we have Christmas trees, why we kiss under the mistletoe, and why Santa Claus visits us every Christmas Eve, and he has made up his own unique stories to answer these questions. Look out for the next book in the series next Christmas!

Christopher would like to thank Frimley Church of England School for reviewing the book pre-publication and for their helpful feedback.

And of course, Christopher would like to thank Emily Harper for her amazing illustrations and he looks forward to working with her on the next book in the *The East Pudding Chronicles*.

ABOUT THE ILLUSTRATOR

Devastated when she didn't receive her Hogwarts letter, Emily decided to do something just as magical so she illustrates and writes children's books instead!

Emily works as an illustrator and animator in Southampton and is currently training to be a primary school teacher. She has worked on a number of other children's books, both writing her own stories and illustrating for other authors.

She found working on *The Christmas Monster* a fantastic excuse to get Christmassy, even though she did do a lot of the drawings on her summer holiday!

Emily would like to give a special thank you to her mum, Julie, who will always be her biggest inspiration.